MATIAS
and the CLOUD

Jorge G. Palomera   Ana Sanfelippo

ETCH
Houghton Mifflin Harcourt
Boston   New York

First U.S. edition.

Text copyright © 2016 by Jorge G. Palomera
Illustrations copyright © 2016 by Ana Sanfelippo
© Bang. ediciones, 2018
English translation rights arranged through S.B.Rights Agency — Stephanie Barrouillet

Etch is an imprint of Houghton Mifflin Harcourt Publishing Company.

hmhbooks.com

The illustrations in this book were done in acrylics, markers, and pencils.
The text was set in Toronto Subway.
Cover design by Kaitlin Yang

Library of Congress Cataloging-in-Publication Data is on file.

ISBN: 978-0-358-46776-2 paperback
ISBN: 978-0-358-46774-8 hardcover

Manufactured in Spain
EP 10 9 8 7 6 5 4 3 2 1
4500836559

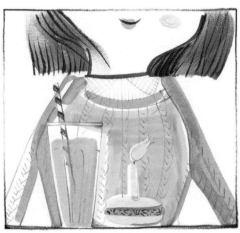

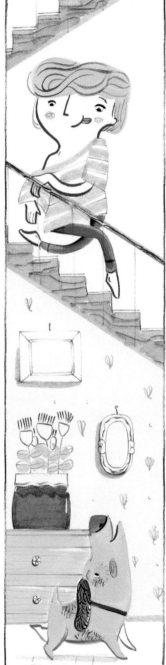

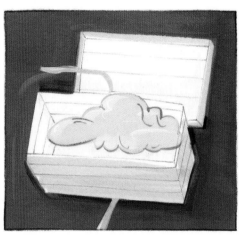

CRASH

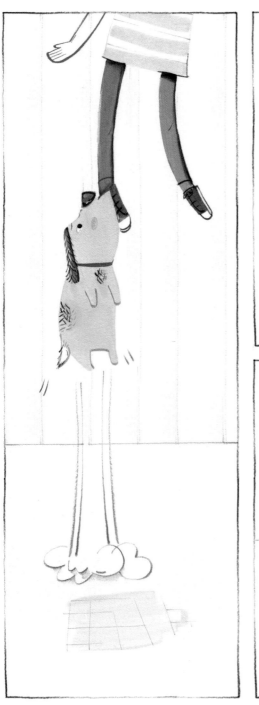